"One of the best." —*The Los Angeles Times*

"Of stories which satisfy our primal appetite for cold shivers along our lumbar regions the best is '**The Beast with Five Fingers**' by W.F. Harvey, a thing manifestly impossible and absurd in daylight, but a story to be avoided by a person alone in a large house at midnight."　　　　　—*The New York Herald*

"A fantastic, blood-curdling and utterly original horror story."
　　　　　—Alison Smith, *The San Francisco Examiner*

"A really admirable ghost story, the gruesome tale of '**The Beast with Five Fingers**.'"　　　　　—*Evening Public Ledger*

"Uncanny and repulsive, but absorbing at the same time."
　　　　　—*The Indianapolis News*

"'**The Beast with Five Fingers**,' told by Mr. W.F. Harvey, is admirably done, with a vivid sense of reserve force which reminds one of Edgar Allen Poe. The cumulative effect of horror is finely managed."　　　　　—*The Daily Telegraph*

"No one who reads the opening chapter will be content until he has reached the end."　　　　　—*The Evening Standard*

"If, like so many readers, one wants the frankly horrible, it is to be found in '**The Beast with Five Fingers**' by W.F. Harvey."
　　　　　—*The Observer*

"When, however, one is convinced he is reading merely an amusing satire he suddenly finds himself in the grip of a thrilling ghost story on the order of de Maupassant, [who], unlike Poe, is never utterly lawless. He assumes one impossible fact and then proceeds to unfold his story in a thoroughly scientific and convincing fashion. W.F. Harvey has the same terrifying habit of creating something monstrous, but law-abiding; an evil spirit, quite in the German manner. It is to be regretted, however, that only a shrewd person will know when to stop laughing and when to be scared."　　　　　—*New York Tribune*

"AND WHAT IN THE NAME OF
ALL THAT'S HOLY IS THAT?"

THE BEAST WITH
FIVE FINGERS
W.F. HARVEY

HEATHEN SHORTS
THEIR STORIES. OUR WAY.

Published in the good ole United States of America
by Heathen Shorts, an imprint of
Heathen Creative
P.O. Box 588
Point Pleasant, WV 25550-0588

Heathen Shorts are available at quantity discounts.
Bear witness to the yackety-yak and tomfoolery at:

heatheneditions.com

Social? Tag us! @heatheneditions
Photo? Tag it! #heathenedition #heathenshort

Caution: This story may alter your mind.

First published in Vol. 1 of *The New Decameron* 1919
First collected in *The Beast with Five Fingers and Other Tales* 1928
Heathen Short published January 5, 2026

Book and cover design by Sheridan Cleland
Set in 10.5pt Scotch Text
Titles in Edirne

ISBN: 979-8-90075-005-7

HEATHEN SHORT #5
FIRST EDITION

"BOTHER IT!
THE BEAST'S GOT OUT."

HEATHENRY:
THOUGHTS ON THE TEXT

Two proper English gentlemen grappling with a maniacal disembodied hand that has a mind of its own—what a fun, wacky, macabre romp this story is!

It was first published in 1919 in Volume 1 of *The New Decameron*, a multi-volume anthology of early 20th-century English short fiction modeled explicitly on Italian author Giovanni Boccaccio's *Decameron*, the famous 14th-century cycle of one hundred tales. Its next appearance was in Harvey's own 1928 collection *The Beast with Five Fingers and Other Tales*.

The story later served as the basis for the 1946 mystery-horror film *The Beast with Five Fingers*, starring a scrumptious Andrea King and the always-creepy Peter Lorre. But the film's relation to the text lies mostly in name and basic premise; it steadily abandons the original's supernatural bent in favor of a more grounded whodunit.

And we would certainly be remiss if we didn't situate Harvey within the long lineage of disembodied hands . . .

Modern readers will think first of Thing from *The Addams Family*, Ash's diabolical severed hand in *Evil Dead II*, or—if you were a child of the 90s—the gleefully chaotic movie *Idle Hands*.

But Harvey himself was obviously drawing from older tales, such as Irish author J. Sheridan Le Fanu's 1863 "An Authentic Narrative of the Ghost of a Hand" or French author Guy de Maupassant's terrifying 1883 short *"La Main"* ("The Hand").

And if these *ahem* *handful* of mentions aren't enough to satisfy you, then how about an entire book (!) devoted to the literary motif of severed hands? *Dead Hands: Fictions of Agency, Renaissance to Modern*, by American scholar Katherine Rowe, traces the familiar Gothic convention of severed hands from early English drama through modern American fiction, mapping the dynamic history of this uncanny device with academic precision and narrative verve.

As for the text itself: because Harvey was English, we have retained his British spellings, though we have updated a handful of archaic hyphenations—good-by becomes goodbye, to-morrow becomes tomorrow, and so on. Our real labor, however, lies in the 55 footnotes we've appended throughout the story to provide clarity, context, and commentary where necessary.

All in all, we believe our additions have rendered this story— if we may borrow an English gentlemanly phrase—jolly good!

Cheers!

THE BEAST WITH FIVE FINGERS

When I was a little boy I once went with my father to call on Adrian Borlsover. I played on the floor with a black spaniel[1] while my father appealed for a subscription.[2] Just before we left my father said, "Mr. Borlsover, may my son here shake hands with you? It will be a thing to look back upon with pride when he grows to be a man."

I came up to the bed on which the old man was lying and put my hand in his, awed by the still beauty of his face. He spoke to me kindly, and hoped that I should always try to please my father. Then he placed his right hand on my head and asked for a blessing to rest upon me. "Amen!" said my father, and I followed him out of the room, feeling as if I wanted to cry. But my father was in excellent spirits.

"That old gentleman, Jim," said he, "is the most wonderful man in the whole town. For ten years he has been quite blind."

"But I saw his eyes," I said. "They were ever so black and shiny; they weren't shut up like Nora's puppies. Can't he see at all?"

And so I learnt for the first time that a man might have eyes

---

[1] A breed of sporting dog with long drooping ears and a wavy, silky coat.
[2] In this context, a contribution to a fund or cause.

that looked dark and beautiful and shining without being able to see.

"Just like Mrs. Tomlinson has big ears," I said, "and can't hear at all except when Mr. Tomlinson shouts."

"Jim," said my father, "it's not right to talk about a lady's ears. Remember what Mr. Borlsover said about pleasing me and being a good boy."

That was the only time I saw Adrian Borlsover. I soon forgot about him and the hand which he laid in blessing on my head. But for a week I prayed that those dark tender eyes might see.

"His spaniel may have puppies," I said in my prayers, "and he will never be able to know how funny they look with their eyes all closed up. Please let old Mr. Borlsover see."

Adrian Borlsover, as my father had said, was a wonderful man. He came of an eccentric family. Borlsovers' sons, for some reason, always seemed to marry very ordinary women, which perhaps accounted for the fact that no Borlsover had been a genius, and only one Borlsover had been mad. But they were great champions of little causes, generous patrons of odd sciences, founders of querulous[3] sects, trustworthy guides to the bypath[4] meadows of erudition.[5]

Adrian was an authority on the fertilization of orchids. He had held at one time the family living at Borlsover Conyers, until a congenital weakness of the lungs obliged him to seek a less rigorous climate in the sunny south coast watering-place where I had seen him. Occasionally he would relieve one or

[3] Complaining or whiny.
[4] Indirect or little-used.
[5] Profound scholarly knowledge acquired by study and research.

other of the local clergy. My father described him as a fine preacher, who gave long and inspiring sermons from what many men would have considered unprofitable texts. "An excellent proof," he would add, "of the truth of the doctrine of direct verbal inspiration."

Adrian Borlsover was exceedingly clever with his hands. His penmanship was exquisite. He illustrated all his scientific papers, made his own woodcuts, and carved the reredos[6] that is at present the chief feature of interest in the church at Borlsover Conyers. He had an exceedingly clever knack in cutting silhouettes for young ladies and paper pigs and cows for little children, and made more than one complicated wind instrument of his own devising.

When he was fifty years old Adrian Borlsover lost his sight. In a wonderfully short time he had adapted himself to the new conditions of life. He quickly learned to read Braille.[7] So marvelous indeed was his sense of touch that he was still able to maintain his interest in botany. The mere passing of his long supple fingers over a flower was sufficient means for its identification, though occasionally he would use his lips. I have found several letters of his among my father's correspondence. In no case was there anything to show that he was afflicted with blindness and this in spite of the fact that he exercised undue economy in the spacing of lines. Toward the close of his life the old man was credited with powers of touch that seemed almost uncanny: it has been said that he could tell at once the color of a ribbon placed between his fingers. My father would neither confirm nor deny the story.

---

[6] A decorative, ornamental screen covering the wall behind an altar.

[7] A form of written language used by blind or visually impaired people in which characters are represented by patterns of raised dots that are felt with the fingertips, created by French educator Louis Braille (1809–1852).

Adrian Borlsover was a bachelor. His elder brother George had married late in life, leaving one son, Eustace, who lived in the gloomy Georgian[1] mansion at Borlsover Conyers, where he could work undisturbed in collecting material for his great book on heredity.

Like his uncle, he was a remarkable man. The Borlsovers had always been born naturalists, but Eustace possessed in a special degree the power of systematizing his knowledge. He had received his university education in Germany, and then, after post-graduate work in Vienna[2] and Naples,[3] had traveled for four years in South America and the East, getting together a huge store of material for a new study into the processes of variation.

He lived alone at Borlsover Conyers with Saunders his secretary, a man who bore a somewhat dubious reputation in the district, but whose powers as a mathematician, combined with his business abilities, were invaluable to Eustace.

---

[1] Georgian architecture is the name given to the set of architectural styles named after the first four British monarchs of the House of Hanover—George I, George II, George III, and George IV—who reigned in continuous succession from 1714 to 1830. It is a classical style known for elegant symmetry, balanced proportions, and heavily influenced by Greek and Roman design, using materials like brick or stone with multi-pane sash windows and classical details like columns and pediments.

[2] The capital of Austria.

[3] A port city on the western coast of Italy.

Uncle and nephew saw little of each other. The visits of Eustace were confined to a week in the summer or autumn: long weeks, that dragged almost as slowly as the bath-chair[4] in which the old man was drawn along the sunny sea front. In their way the two men were fond of each other, though their intimacy would doubtless have been greater had they shared the same religious views. Adrian held to the old-fashioned evangelical dogmas of his early manhood; his nephew for many years had been thinking of embracing Buddhism. Both men possessed, too, the reticence the Borlsovers had always shown, and which their enemies sometimes called hypocrisy. With Adrian it was a reticence as to the things he had left undone; but with Eustace it seemed that the curtain which he was so careful to leave undrawn hid something more than a half-empty chamber.

Two years before his death Adrian Borlsover developed, unknown to himself, the not uncommon power of automatic writing. Eustace made the discovery by accident. Adrian was sitting reading in bed, the forefinger of his left hand tracing the Braille characters, when his nephew noticed that a pencil the old man held in his right hand was moving slowly along the opposite page. He left his seat in the window and sat down beside the bed. The right hand continued to move, and now he could see plainly that they were letters and words which it was forming.

"Adrian Borlsover," wrote the hand, "Eustace Borlsover, George Borlsover, Francis Borlsover, Sigismund Borlsover, Adrian Borlsover, Eustace Borlsover, Saville Borlsover. B, for Borlsover. Honesty is the Best Policy. Beautiful Belinda Borlsover."

---

[4] A hooded wheelchair.

"What curious nonsense!" said Eustace to himself.

"King George the Third[5] ascended the throne in 1760," wrote the hand. "Crowd, a noun of multitude; a collection of individuals—Adrian Borlsover, Eustace Borlsover."

"It seems to me," said his uncle, closing the book, "that you had much better make the most of the afternoon sunshine and take your walk now."

"I think perhaps I will," Eustace answered as he picked up the volume. "I won't go far, and when I come back I can read to you those articles in *Nature*[6] about which we were speaking."

He went along the promenade,[7] but stopped at the first shelter, and seating himself in the corner best protected from the wind, he examined the book at leisure. Nearly every page was scored with a meaningless jungle of pencil marks: rows of capital letters, short words, long words, complete sentences, copybook[8] tags. The whole thing, in fact, had the appearance of a copybook, and on a more careful scrutiny Eustace thought that there was ample evidence to show that the handwriting at the beginning of the book, good though it was was not nearly so good as the handwriting at the end.

He left his uncle at the end of October, with a promise to return early in December. It seemed to him quite clear that the old man's power of automatic writing was developing rapidly, and for the first time he looked forward to a visit that combined duty with interest.

But on his return he was at first disappointed. His uncle, he thought, looked older. He was listless too, preferring others to read to him and dictating nearly all his letters. Not until the day

---

[5] George III, George William Frederick (1738–1820) was King of Great Britain and Ireland from 1760 until his death in 1820.

[6] Founded in 1869, *Nature* is a British weekly scientific journal that features peer-reviewed research from a variety of academic disciplines.

[7] A paved public walkway.

[8] A book of handwriting examples for students to imitate.

before he left had Eustace an opportunity of observing Adrian Borlsover's new-found faculty.

The old man, propped up in bed with pillows, had sunk into a light sleep. His two hands lay on the coverlet, his left hand tightly clasping his right. Eustace took an empty manuscript book and placed a pencil within reach of the fingers of the right hand. They snatched at it eagerly; then dropped the pencil to unloose the left hand from its restraining grasp.

"Perhaps to prevent interference I had better hold that hand," said Eustace to himself, as he watched the pencil. Almost immediately it began to write.

"Blundering Borlsovers, unnecessarily unnatural, extraordinarily eccentric, culpably curious."

"Who are you?" asked Eustace, in a low voice.

"Never you mind," wrote the hand of Adrian.

"Is it my uncle who is writing?"

"Oh, my prophetic soul, mine uncle."

"Is it anyone I know?"

"Silly Eustace, you'll see me very soon."

"When shall I see you?"

"When poor old Adrian's dead."

"Where shall I see you?"

"Where shall you not?"

Instead of speaking his next question, Borlsover wrote it. "What is the time?"

The fingers dropped the pencil and moved three or four times across the paper. Then, picking up the pencil, they wrote:

"Ten minutes before four. Put your book away, Eustace. Adrian mustn't find us working at this sort of thing. He doesn't know what to make of it, and I won't have poor old Adrian disturbed. *Au revoir.*"[9]

---

[9] French: goodbye.

Adrian Borlsover awoke with a start.

"I've been dreaming again," he said; "such queer dreams of leaguered[10] cities and forgotten towns. You were mixed up in this one, Eustace, though I can't remember how. Eustace, I want to warn you. Don't walk in doubtful paths. Choose your friends well. Your poor grandfather——"

A fit of coughing put an end to what he was saying, but Eustace saw that the hand was still writing. He managed unnoticed to draw the book away. "I'll light the gas," he said, "and ring for tea." On the other side of the bed curtain he saw the last sentences that had been written.

"It's too late, Adrian," he read. "We're friends already; aren't we, Eustace Borlsover?"

On the following day Eustace Borlsover left. He thought his uncle looked ill when he said goodbye, and the old man spoke despondently of the failure his life had been.

"Nonsense, uncle!" said his nephew. "You have got over your difficulties in a way not one in a hundred thousand would have done. Everyone marvels at your splendid perseverance in teaching your hand to take the place of your lost sight. To me it's been a revelation of the possibilities of education."

"Education," said his uncle dreamily, as if the word had started a new train of thought, "education is good so long as you know to whom and for what purpose you give it. But with the lower orders of men, the base and more sordid spirits, I have grave doubts as to its results. Well, goodbye, Eustace, I may not see you again. You are a true Borlsover, with all the Borlsover faults. Marry, Eustace. Marry some good, sensible girl. And if by any chance I don't see you again, my will is at my solicitor's.[11] I've not left you any legacy, because I know you're

---

[10] Besieged or surrounded by an army.
[11] In England, a solicitor is an attorney or lawyer.

well provided for, but I thought you might like to have my books. Oh, and there's just one other thing. You know, before the end people often lose control over themselves and make absurd requests. Don't pay any attention to them, Eustace. Goodbye!" and he held out his hand. Eustace took it. It remained in his a fraction of a second longer than he had expected, and gripped him with a virility that was surprising. There was, too, in its touch a subtle sense of intimacy.

"Why, uncle!" he said, "I shall see you alive and well for many long years to come."

Two months later Adrian Borlsover died.

||

Eustace Borlsover was in Naples at the time. He read the obituary notice in the *Morning Post* on the day announced for the funeral.

"Poor old fellow!" he said. "I wonder where I shall find room for all his books."

The question occurred to him again with greater force when three days later he found himself standing in the library at Borlsover Conyers, a huge room built for use, and not for beauty, in the year of Waterloo by a Borlsover who was an ardent admirer of the great Napoleon.[1] It was arranged on the plan of many college libraries, with tall, projecting bookcases forming deep recesses of dusty silence, fit graves for the old hates of forgotten controversy, the dead passions of forgotten lives. At the end of the room, behind the bust of some unknown eighteenth-century divine,[2] an ugly iron corkscrew stair led to a shelf-lined gallery. Nearly every shelf was full.

"I must talk to Saunders about it," said Eustace. "I suppose that it will be necessary to have the billiard-room fitted up with bookcases."

---

[1] The Battle of Waterloo was fought on June 18, 1815, near the village of Waterloo (in what is now Belgium), in which Napoleon's army was defeated by the British and Prussians.

[2] In this context, "divine" means a theologian or clergyman.

The two men met for the first time after many weeks in the dining-room that evening.

"Hullo!" said Eustace, standing before the fire with his hands in his pockets. "How goes the world, Saunders? Why these dress togs?"[3] He himself was wearing an old shooting-jacket. He did not believe in mourning, as he had told his uncle on his last visit; and though he usually went in for quiet-colored ties, he wore this evening one of an ugly red, in order to shock Morton the butler, and to make them thrash out the whole question of mourning for themselves in the servants' hall. Eustace was a true Borlsover.

"The world," said Saunders, "goes the same as usual, confoundedly slow. The dress togs are accounted for by an invitation from Captain Lockwood to bridge."

"How are you getting there?"

"I've told your coachman to drive me in your carriage. Any objection?"

"Oh, dear me, no! We've had all things in common for far too many years for me to raise objections at this hour of the day."

"You'll find your correspondence in the library," went on Saunders. "Most of it I've seen to. There are a few private letters I haven't opened. There's also a box with a rat, or something, inside it that came by the evening post.[4] Very likely it's the six-toed albino. I didn't look, because I didn't want to mess up my things but I should gather from the way it's jumping about that it's pretty hungry."

"Oh, I'll see to it," said Eustace, "while you and the Captain earn an honest penny."

Dinner over and Saunders gone, Eustace went into the

---

[3] Clothes.
[4] Mail.

library. Though the fire had been lit the room was by no means cheerful.

"We'll have all the lights on at any rate," he said, as he turned the switches. "And, Morton," he added, when the butler brought the coffee, "get me a screwdriver or something to undo this box. Whatever the animal is, he's kicking up the deuce of a row.[5] What is it? Why are you dawdling?"

"If you please, sir, when the postman brought it he told me that they'd bored the holes in the lid at the post-office. There were no breathin' holes in the lid, sir, and they didn't want the animal to die. That is all, sir."

"It's culpably careless of the man, whoever he was," said Eustace, as he removed the screws, "packing an animal like this in a wooden box with no means of getting air. Confound it all! I meant to ask Morton to bring me a cage to put it in. Now I suppose I shall have to get one myself."

He placed a heavy book on the lid from which the screws had been removed, and went into the billiard-room. As he came back into the library with an empty cage in his hand he heard the sound of something falling, and then of something scuttling along the floor.

"Bother it! The beast's got out. How in the world am I to find it again in this library!"

To search for it did indeed seem hopeless. He tried to follow the sound of the scuttling in one of the recesses where the animal seemed to be running behind the books in the shelves, but it was impossible to locate it. Eustace resolved to go on quietly reading. Very likely the animal might gain confidence and show itself. Saunders seemed to have dealt in his usual methodical manner with most of the correspondence. There were still the private letters.

---

[5] In this context, a row is a loud commotion or disturbance, and deuce is used as an intensifier.

What was that? Two sharp clicks and the lights in the hideous candelabra[6] that hung from the ceiling suddenly went out.

"I wonder if something has gone wrong with the fuse," said Eustace, as he went to the switches by the door. Then he stopped. There was a noise at the other end of the room, as if something was crawling up the iron corkscrew stair. "If it's gone into the gallery," he said, "well and good." He hastily turned on the lights, crossed the room, and climbed up the stair. But he could see nothing. His grandfather had placed a little gate at the top of the stair, so that children could run and romp in the gallery without fear of accident. This Eustace closed, and having considerably narrowed the circle of his search, returned to his desk by the fire.

How gloomy the library was! There was no sense of intimacy about the room. The few busts that an eighteenth-century Borlsover had brought back from the grand tour, might have been in keeping in the old library. Here they seemed out of place. They made the room feel cold, in spite of the heavy red damask[7] curtains and great gilt cornices.[8]

With a crash two heavy books fell from the gallery to the floor; then, as Borlsover looked, another and yet another.

"Very well; you'll starve for this, my beauty!" he said. "We'll do some little experiments on the metabolism of rats deprived of water. Go on! Chuck them down! I think I've got the upper hand." He turned once again to his correspondence. The letter was from the family solicitor. It spoke of his uncle's death and of the valuable collection of books that had been left to him in the will.

"There was one request," he read, "which certainly came as a surprise to me. As you know, Mr. Adrian Borlsover had

---

[6] An ornate candleholder with several arms or branches.

[7] Woven fabric whose pattern is visible on both sides.

[8] A cornice is an ornamental molding at the top of a wall just below the ceiling. Gilt means that it is covered with gold leaf or gold paint.

left instructions that his body was to be buried in as simple a manner as possible at Eastbourne.[9] He expressed a desire that there should be neither wreaths nor flowers of any kind, and hoped that his friends and relatives would not consider it necessary to wear mourning. The day before his death we received a letter canceling these instructions. He wished his body to be embalmed (he gave us the address of the man we were to employ—Pennifer, Ludgate Hill), with orders that his right hand was to be sent to you, stating that it was at your special request. The other arrangements as to the funeral remained unaltered."

"Good Lord!" said Eustace; "what in the world was the old boy driving at? And what in the name of all that's holy is that?"

Someone was in the gallery. Someone had pulled the cord attached to one of the blinds, and it had rolled up with a snap. Someone must be in the gallery, for a second blind did the same. Someone must be walking round the gallery, for one after the other the blinds sprang up, letting in the moonlight.

"I haven't got to the bottom of this yet," said Eustace, "but I will do before the night is very much older," and he hurried up the corkscrew stair. He had just got to the top when the lights went out a second time, and he heard again the scuttling along the floor. Quickly he stole on tiptoe in the dim moonshine in the direction of the noise, feeling as he went for one of the switches. His fingers touched the metal knob at last. He turned on the electric light.

About ten yards in front of him, crawling along the floor, was a man's hand. Eustace stared at it in utter astonishment. It was moving quickly, in the manner of a geometer caterpillar,[10] the fingers humped up one moment, flattened out the next; the thumb appeared to give a crab-like motion to the whole. While

---

[9] A town and seaside resort on the south coast of England.

[10] An inchworm. Specifically, a geometrid belonging to the family Geometridae.

he was looking, too surprised to stir, the hand disappeared round the corner. Eustace ran forward. He no longer saw it, but he could hear it as it squeezed its way behind the books on one of the shelves. A heavy volume had been displaced. There was a gap in the row of books where it had got in. In his fear lest it should escape him again, he seized the first book that came to his hand and plugged it into the hole. Then, emptying two shelves of their contents, he took the wooden boards and propped them up in front to make his barrier doubly sure.

"I wish Saunders was back," he said; "one can't tackle this sort of thing alone." It was after eleven, and there seemed little likelihood of Saunders returning before twelve. He did not dare to leave the shelf unwatched, even to run downstairs to ring the bell. Morton the butler often used to come round about eleven to see that the windows were fastened, but he might not come. Eustace was thoroughly unstrung. At last he heard steps down below.

"Morton!" he shouted; "Morton!"

"Sir?"

"Has Mr. Saunders got back yet?"

"Not yet, sir."

"Well, bring me some brandy, and hurry up about it. I'm up here in the gallery, you duffer."[11]

"Thanks," said Eustace, as he emptied the glass. "Don't go to bed yet, Morton. There are a lot of books that have fallen down by accident; bring them up and put them back in their shelves."

Morton had never seen Borlsover in so talkative a mood as on that night. "Here," said Eustace, when the books had been put back and dusted, "you might hold up these boards for me, Morton. That beast in the box got out, and I've been chasing it all over the place."

---

[11] Incompetent person.

"I think I can hear it chawing[12] at the books, sir. They're not valuable, I hope? I think that's the carriage, sir; I'll go and call Mr. Saunders."

It seemed to Eustace that he was away for five minutes, but it could hardly have been more than one when he returned with Saunders. "All right, Morton, you can go now. I'm up here, Saunders."

"What's all the row?" asked Saunders, as he lounged forward with his hands in his pockets. The luck had been with him all the evening. He was completely satisfied, both with himself and with Captain Lockwood's taste in wines. "What's the matter? You look to me to be in an absolute blue funk."

"That old devil of an uncle of mine," began Eustace—"oh, I can't explain it all. It's his hand that's been playing old Harry all the evening.[13] But I've got it cornered behind these books. You've got to help me catch it."

"What's up with you, Eustace? What's the game?"

"It's no game, you silly idiot! If you don't believe me take out one of those books and put your hand in and feel."

"All right," said Saunders; "but wait till I've rolled up my sleeve. The accumulated dust of centuries, eh?" He took off his coat, knelt down, and thrust his arm along the shelf.

"There's something there right enough," he said. "It's got a funny stumpy end to it, whatever it is, and nips like a crab. Ah, no, you don't!" He pulled his hand out in a flash. "Shove in a book quickly. Now it can't get out."

"What was it?" asked Eustace.

"It was something that wanted very much to get hold of me. I felt what seemed like a thumb and forefinger. Give me some brandy."

---

[12] Chewing.

[13] "Playing old Harry" — a euphemistic term for the devil — means to ruin, destroy, cause trouble, or make a mess of something.

"How are we to get it out of there?"

"What about a landing net?"[14]

"No good. It would be too smart for us. I tell you, Saunders, it can cover the ground far faster than I can walk. But I think I see how we can manage it. The two books at the end of the shelf are big ones that go right back against the wall. The others are very thin. I'll take out one at a time, and you slide the rest along until we have it squashed between the end two."

It certainly seemed to be the best plan. One by one, as they took out the books, the space behind grew smaller and smaller. There was something in it that was certainly very much alive. Once they caught sight of fingers pressing outward for a way of escape. At last they had it pressed between the two big books.

"There's muscle there, if there isn't flesh and blood," said Saunders, as he held them together. "It seems to be a hand right enough, too. I suppose this is a sort of infectious hallucination. I've read about such cases before."

"Infectious fiddlesticks!"[15] said Eustace, his face white with anger; "bring the thing downstairs. We'll get it back into the box."

It was not altogether easy, but they were successful at last. "Drive in the screws," said Eustace, "we won't run any risks. Put the box in this old desk of mine. There's nothing in it that I want. Here's the key. Thank goodness, there's nothing wrong with the lock."

"Quite a lively evening," said Saunders. "Now let's hear more about your uncle."

They sat up together until early morning. Saunders had no desire for sleep. Eustace was trying to explain and to forget: to conceal from himself a fear that he had never felt before—the fear of walking alone down the long corridor to his bedroom.

---

[14] A long-handled net for lifting hooked fish from water.
[15] Nonsense.

"Whatever it was," said Eustace to Saunders on the following morning, "I propose that we drop the subject. There's nothing to keep us here for the next ten days. We'll motor up to the Lakes and get some climbing."

"And see nobody all day, and sit bored to death with each other every night. Not for me thanks. Why not run up to town? Run's the exact word in this case, isn't it? We're both in such a blessed funk. Pull yourself together Eustace, and let's have another look at the hand."

"As you like," said Eustace; "there's the key." They went into the library and opened the desk. The box was as they had left it on the previous night.

"What are you waiting for?" asked Eustace.

"I am waiting for you to volunteer to open the lid. However, since you seem to funk[1] it, allow me. There doesn't seem to be the likelihood of any rumpus this morning, at all events." He opened the lid and picked out the hand.

"Cold?" asked Eustace.

"Tepid. A bit below blood-heat by the feel. Soft and supple

[1] In this context, fear.

too. If it's the embalming, it's a sort of embalming I've never seen before. Is it your uncle's hand?"

"Oh, yes, it's his all right," said Eustace. "I should know those long thin fingers anywhere. Put it back in the box, Saunders. Never mind about the screws. I'll lock the desk, so that there'll be no chance of its getting out. We'll compromise by motoring up to town for a week. If we get off soon after lunch we ought to be at Grantham[2] or Stamford[3] by night."

"Right," said Saunders; "and tomorrow—Oh, well, by tomorrow we shall have forgotten all about this beastly thing."

If when the morrow came they had not forgotten, it was certainly true that at the end of the week they were able to tell a very vivid ghost story at the little supper Eustace gave on Hallow E'en.[4]

"You don't want us to believe that it's true, Mr. Borlsover? How perfectly awful!"

"I'll take my oath on it, and so would Saunders here; wouldn't you, old chap?"

"Any number of oaths," said Saunders. "It was a long thin hand, you know, and it gripped me just like that."

"Don't Mr. Saunders! Don't! How perfectly horrid! Now tell us another one, do. Only a really creepy one, please!"

"Here's a pretty mess!" said Eustace on the following day as

[2] A town and civil parish in the South Kesteven district of Lincolnshire, England.

[3] A town and civil parish also in Lincolnshire, approximately 22 miles (36 km) from Grantham.

[4] An older rendering of Halloween, a contraction of All Hallows' Eve (the name refers to the evening before All Saints' Day, November 1st); "E'en" is a poetic or archaic abbreviation for "evening."

he threw a letter across the table to Saunders. "It's your affair, though. Mrs. Merrit, if I understand it, gives a month's notice."

"Oh, that's quite absurd on Mrs. Merrit's part," Saunders replied. "She doesn't know what she's talking about. Let's see what she says."

"Dear Sir," he read, "this is to let you know that I must give you a month's notice as from Tuesday the 13th. For a long time I've felt the place too big for me, but when Jane Parfit, and Emma Laidlaw go off with scarcely as much as an 'if you please,' after frightening the wits out of the other girls, so that they can't turn out a room by themselves or walk alone down the stairs for fear of treading on half-frozen toads or hearing it run along the passages at night, all I can say is that it's no place for me. So I must ask you, Mr. Borlsover, sir, to find a new housekeeper that has no objection to large and lonely houses, which some people do say, not that I believe them for a minute, my poor mother always having been a Wesleyan,[5] are haunted.

"Yours faithfully,

"Elizabeth Merrit.

"P.S.—I should be obliged if you would give my respects to Mr. Saunders. I hope that he won't run no risks with his cold."

"Saunders," said Eustace, "you've always had a wonderful way with you in dealing with servants. You mustn't let poor old Merrit go."

"Of course she shan't go," said Saunders. "She's probably only angling for a rise in salary. I'll write to her this morning."

"No; there's nothing like a personal interview. We've had

---

[5] A Methodist; the name derives from John Wesley (1703–1791), an English cleric, theologian, and evangelist who founded the Methodist Church.

enough of town. We'll go back tomorrow, and you must work your cold for all it's worth. Don't forget that it's got on to the chest, and will require weeks of feeding up and nursing."

"All right. I think I can manage Mrs. Merrit."

But Mrs. Merrit was more obstinate than he had thought. She was very sorry to hear of Mr. Saunders's cold, and how he lay awake all night in London coughing; very sorry indeed. She'd change his room for him gladly, and get the south room aired. And wouldn't he have a basin of hot bread and milk last thing at night? But she was afraid that she would have to leave at the end of the month.

"Try her with an increase of salary," was the advice of Eustace.

It was no use. Mrs. Merrit was obdurate,[6] though she knew of a Mrs. Handyside who had been housekeeper to Lord Gargrave, who might be glad to come at the salary mentioned.

"What's the matter with the servants, Morton?" asked Eustace that evening when he brought the coffee into the library. "What's all this about Mrs. Merrit wanting to leave?"

"If you please, sir, I was going to mention it myself. I have a confession to make, sir. When I found your note asking me to open that desk and take out the box with the rat, I broke the lock as you told me, and was glad to do it, because I could hear the animal in the box making a great noise, and I thought it wanted food. So I took out the box, sir, and got a cage, and was going to transfer it, when the animal got away."

"What in the world are you talking about? I never wrote any such note."

"Excuse me, sir, it was the note I picked up here on the floor on the day you and Mr. Saunders left. I have it in my pocket now."

---

[6] Stubborn.

It certainly seemed to be in Eustace's handwriting. It was written in pencil, and began somewhat abruptly.

"Get a hammer, Morton," he read, "or some other tool, and break open the lock in the old desk in the library. Take out the box that is inside. You need not do anything else. The lid is already open. Eustace Borlsover."

"And you opened the desk?"

"Yes, sir; and as I was getting the cage ready the animal hopped out."

"What animal?"

"The animal inside the box, sir."

"What did it look like?"

"Well, sir, I couldn't tell you," said Morton nervously; "my back was turned, and it was halfway down the room when I looked up."

"What was its color?" asked Saunders; "black?"

"Oh, no, sir, a grayish white. It crept along in a very funny way, sir. I don't think it had a tail."

"What did you do then?"

"I tried to catch it, but it was no use. So I set the rat-traps and kept the library shut. Then that girl Emma Laidlaw left the door open when she was cleaning, and I think it must have escaped."

"And you think it was the animal that's been frightening the maids?"

"Well, no, sir, not quite. They said it was—you'll excuse me, sir—a hand that they saw. Emma trod on it once at the bottom of the stairs. She thought then it was a half-frozen toad, only white. And then Parfit was washing up the dishes in the scullery.[7] She wasn't thinking about anything in particular. It was close on dusk. She took her hands out of the water and was drying them

---

[7] A small room adjoining the kitchen in British homes of the past.

absent-minded like on the roller towel, when she found that she was drying someone else's hand as well, only colder than hers."

"What nonsense!" exclaimed Saunders.

"Exactly, sir; that's what I told her; but we couldn't get her to stop."

"You don't believe all this?" said Eustace, turning suddenly toward the butler.

"Me, sir? Oh, no, sir! I've not seen anything."

"Nor heard anything?"

"Well, sir, if you must know, the bells do ring at odd times, and there's nobody there when we go; and when we go round to draw the blinds of a night, as often as not somebody's been there before us. But as I says to Mrs. Merrit, a young monkey might do wonderful things, and we all know that Mr. Borlsover has had some strange animals about the place."

"Very well, Morton, that will do."

"What do you make of it?" asked Saunders when they were alone. "I mean of the letter he said you wrote."

"Oh, that's simple enough," said Eustace. "See the paper it's written on? I stopped using that years ago, but there were a few odd sheets and envelopes left in the old desk. We never fastened up the lid of the box before locking it in. The hand got out, found a pencil, wrote this note, and shoved it through a crack on to the floor where Morton found it. That's plain as daylight."

"But the hand couldn't write?"

"Couldn't it? You've not seen it do the things I've seen," and he told Saunders more of what had happened at Eastbourne.

"Well," said Saunders, "in that case we have at least an explanation of the legacy. It was the hand which wrote unknown to your uncle that letter to your solicitor, bequeathing itself to you. Your uncle had no more to do with that request than I. In fact, it would seem that he had some idea of this automatic writing, and feared it."

"Then if it's not my uncle, what is it?"

"I suppose some people might say that a disembodied spirit had got your uncle to educate and prepare a little body for it. Now it's got into that little body and is off on its own."

"Well, what are we to do?"

"We'll keep our eyes open," said Saunders, "and try to catch it. If we can't do that, we shall have to wait till the bally[8] clockwork runs down. After all, if it's flesh and blood, it can't live forever."

For two days nothing happened. Then Saunders saw it sliding down the banister in the hall. He was taken unawares, and lost a full second before he started in pursuit, only to find that the thing had escaped him. Three days later, Eustace, writing alone in the library at night, saw it sitting on an open book at the other end of the room. The fingers crept over the page, feeling the print as if it were reading; but before he had time to get up from his seat, it had taken the alarm and was pulling itself up the curtains. Eustace watched it grimly as it hung onto the cornice with three fingers, flicking thumb and forefinger at him in an expression of scornful derision.

"I know what I'll do," he said. "If I only get it into the open I'll set the dogs on to it."

He spoke to Saunders of the suggestion.

"It's a jolly good idea," he said; "only we won't wait till we find it out of doors. We'll get the dogs. There are the two terriers and the underkeeper's Irish mongrel that's on to rats like a flash. Your spaniel has not got spirit enough for this sort of game." They brought the dogs into the house, and the keeper's Irish mongrel chewed up the slippers, and the terriers tripped up

---

[8] British slang for "bloody."

Morton as he waited at table; but all three were welcome. Even false security is better than no security at all.

For a fortnight[9] nothing happened. Then the hand was caught, not by the dogs, but by Mrs. Merrit's gray parrot. The bird was in the habit of periodically removing the pins that kept its seed and water tins in place, and of escaping through the holes in the side of the cage. When once at liberty Peter would show no inclination to return, and would often be about the house for days. Now, after six consecutive weeks of captivity, Peter had again discovered a new means of unloosing his bolts and was at large, exploring the tapestried forests of the curtains and singing songs in praise of liberty from cornice and picture rail.

"It's no use your trying to catch him," said Eustace to Mrs. Merrit, as she came into the study one afternoon toward dusk with a stepladder. "You'd much better leave Peter alone. Starve him into surrender, Mrs. Merrit, and don't leave bananas and seed about for him to peck at when he fancies he's hungry. You're far too softhearted."

"Well, sir, I see he's right out of reach now on that picture rail, so if you wouldn't mind closing the door, sir, when you leave the room, I'll bring his cage in tonight and put some meat inside it. He's that fond of meat, though it does make him pull out his feathers to suck the quills. They *do* say that if you cook—"

"Never mind, Mrs. Merrit," said Eustace, who was busy writing. "That will do; I'll keep an eye on the bird."

There was silence in the room, unbroken but for the continuous whisper of his pen.

"Scratch poor Peter," said the bird. "Scratch poor old Peter!"

"Be quiet, you beastly bird!"

"Poor old Peter! Scratch poor Peter, do."

---

[9] Two weeks.

"I'm more likely to wring your neck if I get hold of you." He looked up at the picture rail, and there was the hand holding on to a hook with three fingers, and slowly scratching the head of the parrot with the fourth. Eustace ran to the bell and pressed it hard; then across to the window, which he closed with a bang. Frightened by the noise the parrot shook its wings preparatory to flight, and as it did so the fingers of the hand got hold of it by the throat. There was a shrill scream from Peter as he fluttered across the room, wheeling round in circles that ever descended, borne down under the weight that clung to him. The bird dropped at last quite suddenly, and Eustace saw fingers and feathers rolled into an inextricable[10] mass on the floor. The struggle abruptly ceased as finger and thumb squeezed the neck; the bird's eyes rolled up to show the whites, and there was a faint, half-choked gurgle. But before the fingers had time to loose their hold, Eustace had them in his own.

"Send Mr. Saunders here at once," he said to the maid who came in answer to the bell. "Tell him I want him immediately."

Then he went with the hand to the fire. There was a ragged gash across the back where the bird's beak had torn it, but no blood oozed from the wound. He noticed with disgust that the nails had grown long and discolored.

"I'll burn the beastly thing," he said. But he could not burn it. He tried to throw it into the flames, but his own hands, as if restrained by some old primitive feeling, would not let him. And so Saunders found him pale and irresolute, with the hand still clasped tightly in his fingers.

"I've got it at last," he said in a tone of triumph.

"Good; let's have a look at it."

"Not when it's loose. Get me some nails and a hammer and a board of some sort."

---

[10] Impossible to separate.

"Can you hold it all right?"

"Yes, the thing's quite limp; tired out with throttling poor old Peter, I should say."

"And now," said Saunders when he returned with the things, "what are we going to do?"

"Drive a nail through it first, so that it can't get away; then we can take our time over examining it."

"Do it yourself," said Saunders. "I don't mind helping you with guinea-pigs occasionally when there's something to be learned; partly because I don't fear a guinea-pig's revenge. This thing's different."

"All right, you miserable skunk. I won't forget the way you've stood by me."

He took up a nail, and before Saunders had realised what he was doing had driven it through the hand, deep into the board.

"Oh, my aunt," he giggled hysterically, "look at it now," for the hand was writhing in agonized contortions, squirming and wriggling upon the nail like a worm upon the hook.

"Well," said Saunders, "you've done it now. I'll leave you to examine it."

"Don't go, in heaven's name. Cover it up, man, cover it up! Shove a cloth over it! Here!" and he pulled off the antimacassar[11] from the back of a chair and wrapped the board in it. "Now get the keys from my pocket and open the safe. Chuck the other things out. Oh, Lord, it's getting itself into frightful knots! and open it quick!" He threw the thing in and banged the door.

"We'll keep it there till it dies," he said. "May I burn in hell if I ever open the door of that safe again."

---

[11] An ornamental or decorative covering for the back or arms of a chair or sofa to protect it from grease, dirt, and hair oils.

Mrs. Merrit departed at the end of the month. Her successor certainly was more successful in the management of the servants. Early in her rule she declared that she would stand no nonsense, and gossip soon withered and died. Eustace Borlsover went back to his old way of life. Old habits crept over and covered his new experience. He was, if anything, less morose, and showed a greater inclination to take his natural part in country society.

"I shouldn't be surprised if he marries one of these days," said Saunders. "Well, I'm in no hurry for such an event. I know Eustace far too well for the future Mrs. Borlsover to like me. It will be the same old story again: a long friendship slowly made — marriage — and a long friendship quickly forgotten."

IV

But Eustace Borlsover did not follow the advice of his uncle and marry. He was too fond of old slippers and tobacco. The cooking, too, under Mrs. Handyside's management was excellent, and she seemed, too, to have a heaven-sent faculty in knowing when to stop dusting.

Little by little the old life resumed its old power. Then came the burglary. The men, it was said, broke into the house by way of the conservatory.[1] It was really little more than an attempt, for they only succeeded in carrying away a few pieces of plate from the pantry. The safe in the study was certainly found open and empty, but, as Mr. Borlsover informed the police inspector, he had kept nothing of value in it during the last six months.

"Then you're lucky in getting off so easily, sir," the man replied. "By the way they have gone about their business, I should say they were experienced cracksmen.[2] They must have caught the alarm when they were just beginning their evening's work."

"Yes," said Eustace, "I suppose I am lucky."

"I've no doubt," said the inspector, "that we shall be able to trace the men. I've said that they must have been old hands at the game. The way they got in and opened the safe shows that.

---

[1] A greenhouse attached to a house.
[2] Another term for burglars, especially safecrackers.

But there's one little thing that puzzles me. One of them was careless enough not to wear gloves, and I'm bothered if I know what he was trying to do. I've traced his finger-marks on the new varnish on the window sashes in every one of the downstairs rooms. They are very distinct ones too."

"Right hand or left, or both?" asked Eustace.

"Oh, right every time. That's the funny thing. He must have been a foolhardy fellow, and I rather think it was him that wrote that." He took out a slip of paper from his pocket. "That's what he wrote, sir. 'I've got out, Eustace Borlsover, but I'll be back before long.' Some gaol[3] bird just escaped, I suppose. It will make it all the easier for us to trace him. Do you know the writing, sir?"

"No," said Eustace; "it's not the writing of anyone I know."

"I'm not going to stay here any longer," said Eustace to Saunders at luncheon. "I've got on far better during the last six months than ever I expected, but I'm not going to run the risk of seeing that thing again. I shall go up to town this afternoon. Get Morton to put my things together, and join me with the car at Brighton[4] on the day after tomorrow. And bring the proofs of those two papers with you. We'll run over them together."

"How long are you going to be away?"

"I can't say for certain, but be prepared to stay for some time. We've stuck to work pretty closely through the summer, and I for one need a holiday. I'll engage the rooms at Brighton. You'll find it best to break the journey at Hitchin. I'll wire to you there at the Crown to tell you the Brighton address."

The house he chose at Brighton was in a terrace. He had been there before. It was kept by his old college gyp,[5] a man of

[3] British spelling for "jail."
[4] A seaside resort on the southern coast of England.
[5] In this context, a British term for a college servant at the Universities of Cambridge and Durham.

discreet silence, who was admirably partnered by an excellent cook. The rooms were on the first floor. The two bedrooms were at the back, and opened out of each other. "Saunders can have the smaller one, though it is the only one with a fireplace," he said. "I'll stick to the larger of the two, since it's got a bathroom adjoining. I wonder what time he'll arrive with the car."

Saunders came about seven, cold and cross and dirty. "We'll light the fire in the dining-room," said Eustace, "and get Prince to unpack some of the things while we are at dinner. What were the roads like?"

"Rotten; swimming with mud, and a beastly cold wind against us all day. And this is July. Dear old England!"

"Yes," said Eustace, "I think we might do worse than leave dear old England for a few months."

They turned in soon after twelve.

"You oughtn't to feel cold, Saunders," said Eustace, "when you can afford to sport a great cat-skin lined coat like this. You do yourself very well, all things considered. Look at those gloves, for instance. Who could possibly feel cold when wearing them?"

"They are far too clumsy though for driving. Try them on and see," and he tossed them through the door onto Eustace's bed, and went on with his unpacking. A minute later he heard a shrill cry of terror. "Oh, Lord," he heard, "it's in the glove! Quick, Saunders, quick!" Then came a smacking thud. Eustace had thrown it from him. "I've chucked it into the bathroom," he gasped, "it's hit the wall and fallen into the bath. Come now if you want to help." Saunders, with a lighted candle in his hand, looked over the edge of the bath. There it was, old and maimed, dumb and blind, with a ragged hole in the middle, crawling, staggering, trying to creep up the slippery sides, only to fall back helpless.

"Stay there," said Saunders. "I'll empty a collar box[6] or something, and we'll jam it in. It can't get out while I'm away."

"Yes, it can," shouted Eustace. "It's getting out now. It's climbing up the plug chain. No, you brute, you filthy brute, you don't! Come back, Saunders, it's getting away from me. I can't hold it; it's all slippery. Curse its claw! Shut the window, you idiot! The top too, as well as the bottom. You utter idiot! It's got out!" There was the sound of something dropping on to the hard flagstones below, and Eustace fell back fainting.

For a fortnight he was ill.

"I don't know what to make of it," the doctor said to Saunders. "I can only suppose that Mr. Borlsover has suffered some great emotional shock. You had better let me send someone to help you nurse him. And by all means indulge that whim of his never to be left alone in the dark. I would keep a light burning all night if I were you. But he *must* have more fresh air. It's perfectly absurd this hatred of open windows."

Eustace, however, would have no one with him but Saunders. "I don't want the other men," he said. "They'd smuggle it in somehow. I know they would."

"Don't worry about it, old chap. This sort of thing can't go on indefinitely. You know I saw it this time as well as you. It wasn't half so active. It won't go on living much longer, especially after that fall. I heard it hit the flags myself. As soon as you're a bit stronger we'll leave this place; not bag and baggage, but with only the clothes on our backs, so that it won't be able to hide anywhere. We'll escape it that way. We won't give any address,

---

[6] A storage container popular from the late 19th to early 20th centuries, typically round and made of leather, designed to hold and protect detachable shirt collars.

and we won't have any parcels sent after us. Cheer up, Eustace! You'll be well enough to leave in a day or two. The doctor says I can take you out in a chair tomorrow."

"What have I done?" asked Eustace. "Why does it come after me? I'm no worse than other men. I'm no worse than you, Saunders; you know I'm not. It was you who were at the bottom of that dirty business in San Diego, and that was fifteen years ago."

"It's not that, of course," said Saunders. "We are in the twentieth century, and even the parsons[7] have dropped the idea of your old sins finding you out. Before you caught the hand in the library it was filled with pure malevolence[8]—to you and all mankind. After you spiked it through with that nail it naturally forgot about other people, and concentrated its attention on you. It was shut up in the safe, you know, for nearly six months. That gives plenty of time for thinking of revenge."

Eustace Borlsover would not leave his room, but he thought that there might be something in Saunders's suggestion to leave Brighton without notice. He began rapidly to regain his strength.

"We'll go on the first of September," he said.

The evening of August 31st was oppressively warm. Though at midday the windows had been wide open, they had been shut an hour or so before dusk. Mrs. Prince had long since ceased to wonder at the strange habits of the gentlemen on the first floor. Soon after their arrival she had been told to take down the heavy window curtains in the two bedrooms, and day by day the rooms had seemed to grow more bare. Nothing was left lying about.

"Mr. Borlsover doesn't like to have any place where dirt can

---

[7] Members of the clergy, especially Protestant ones.
[8] Evil.

collect," Saunders had said as an excuse. "He likes to see into all the corners of the room."

"Couldn't I open the window just a little?" he said to Eustace that evening. "We're simply roasting in here, you know."

"No, leave well alone. We're not a couple of boarding-school misses fresh from a course of hygiene lectures. Get the chess-board out."

They sat down and played. At ten o'clock Mrs. Prince came to the door with a note. "I am sorry I didn't bring it before," she said, "but it was left in the letterbox."[9]

"Open it, Saunders, and see if it wants answering."

It was very brief. There was neither address nor signature:

"Will eleven o'clock tonight be suitable for our last appointment?"

"Who is it from?" asked Borlsover.

"It was meant for me," said Saunders. "There's no answer, Mrs. Prince," and he put the paper into his pocket. "A dunning[10] letter from a tailor; I suppose he must have got wind of our leaving."

It was a clever lie, and Eustace asked no more questions. They went on with their game.

On the landing outside Saunders could hear the grandfather's clock whispering the seconds, blurting out the quarter-hours.

"Check!" said Eustace. The clock struck eleven. At the same time there was a gentle knocking on the door; it seemed to come from the bottom panel.

"Who's there?" asked Eustace.

There was no answer.

[9] Mailbox.
[10] A demand for payment of debt.

"Mrs. Prince, is that you?"

"She is up above," said Saunders; "I can hear her walking about the room."

"Then lock the door; bolt it too. Your move, Saunders."

While Saunders sat with his eyes on the chessboard, Eustace walked over to the window and examined the fastenings. He did the same in Saunders's room and the bathroom. There were no doors between the three rooms, or he would have shut and locked them too.

"Now, Saunders," he said, "don't stay all night over your move. I've had time to smoke one cigarette already. It's bad to keep an invalid waiting. There's only one possible thing for you to do. What was that?"

"The ivy blowing against the window. There, it's your move now, Eustace."

"It wasn't the ivy, you idiot. It was someone tapping at the window," and he pulled up the blind. On the outer side of the window, clinging to the sash, was the hand.

"What is it that it's holding?"

"It's a pocketknife. It's going to try to open the window by pushing back the fastener with the blade."

"Well, let it try," said Eustace. "Those fasteners screw down; they can't be opened that way. Anyhow, we'll close the shutters. It's your move, Saunders. I've played."

But Saunders found it impossible to fix his attention on the game. He could not understand Eustace, who seemed all at once to have lost his fear. "What do you say to some wine?" he asked. "You seem to be taking things coolly, but I don't mind confessing that I'm in a blessed funk."

"You've no need to be. There's nothing supernatural about that hand, Saunders. I mean it seems to be governed by the laws of time and space. It's not the sort of thing that vanishes into thin air or slides through oaken doors. And since that's so, I defy it to get in here. We'll leave the place in the morning. I for one have bottomed the depths of fear. Fill your glass, man! The windows are all shuttered, the door is locked and bolted. Pledge me my uncle Adrian! Drink, man! What are you waiting for?"

Saunders was standing with his glass half raised. "It can get in," he said hoarsely; "it can get in! We've forgotten. There's the fireplace in my bedroom. It will come down the chimney."

"Quick!" said Eustace, as he rushed into the other room; "we haven't a minute to lose. What can we do? Light the fire, Saunders. Give me a match, quick!"

"They must be all in the other room. I'll get them."

"Hurry, man, for goodness' sake! Look in the bookcase! Look in the bathroom! Here, come and stand here; I'll look."

"Be quick!" shouted Saunders. "I can hear something!"

"Then plug a sheet from your bed up the chimney. No, here's a match." He had found one at last that had slipped into a crack in the floor.

"Is the fire laid? Good, but it may not burn. I know—the oil from that old reading-lamp and this cotton-wool. Now the match, quick! Pull the sheet away, you fool! We don't want it now."

There was a great roar from the grate as the flames shot up. Saunders had been a fraction of a second too late with the sheet. The oil had fallen on to it. It, too, was burning.

"The whole place will be on fire!" cried Eustace, as he tried to beat out the flames with a blanket. "It's no good! I can't manage it. You must open the door, Saunders, and get help."

Saunders ran to the door and fumbled with the bolts. The key was stiff in the lock.

"Hurry!" shouted Eustace; "the whole place is ablaze!"

The key turned in the lock at last. For half a second Saunders stopped to look back. Afterward he could never be quite sure as to what he had seen, but at the time he thought that something black and charred was creeping slowly, very slowly, from the mass of flames toward Eustace Borlsover. For a moment he thought of returning to his friend, but the noise and the smell of the burning sent him running down the passage crying, "Fire! Fire!" He rushed to the telephone to summon help, and then back to the bathroom—he should have thought of that before— for water. As he burst open the bedroom door there came a scream of terror which ended suddenly, and then the sound of a heavy fall.

EPILOGUE

This is the story which I heard on successive Saturday evenings from the senior mathematical master at a second-rate suburban school. For Saunders has had to earn a living in a way which other men might reckon less congenial than his old manner of life. I had mentioned by chance the name of Adrian Borlsover, and wondered at the time why he changed the conversation with such unusual abruptness. A week later, Saunders began to tell me something of his own history—sordid enough, though shielded with a reserve I could well understand, for it had to cover not only his failings but those of a dead friend. Of the final tragedy he was at first especially loath to speak, and it was only gradually that I was able to piece together the narrative of the preceding pages. Saunders was reluctant to draw any conclusions. At one time he thought that the fingered beast had been animated by the spirit of Sigismund Borlsover, a sinister eighteenth-century ancestor, who, according to legend, built and worshipped in the ugly pagan temple that overlooked the lake. At another time Saunders believed the spirit to belong to a man whom Eustace had once employed as a laboratory assistant, "a black-haired spiteful little brute," he said, "who died cursing his doctor because the fellow couldn't help him to live to settle some paltry score with Borlsover."

From the point of view of direct contemporary evidence, Saunders's story is practically uncorroborated. All the letters mentioned in the narrative were destroyed, with the exception of the last note which Eustace received, or rather which he would have received had not Saunders intercepted it. That I have seen myself. The handwriting was thin and shaky, the handwriting of an old man. I remember the Greek "e" was used in "appointment." A little thing that amused me at the time was that Saunders seemed to keep the note pressed between the pages of his Bible.

I had seen Adrian Borlsover once. Saunders, I learnt to know well. It was by chance, however, and not by design, that I met a third person of the story, Morton the butler. Saunders and I were walking in the Zoological Gardens[1] one Sunday afternoon, when he called my attention to an old man who was standing before the door of the reptile house.

"Why, Morton!" he said, clapping him on the back. "How is the world treating you?"

"Poorly, Mr. Saunders," said the old fellow, though his face lighted up at the greeting.

"The winters drag terribly nowadays. There don't seem no summers or springs."

"You haven't found what you were looking for, I suppose?"

"No, sir, not yet; but I shall do some day. I always told them that Mr. Borlsover kept some queer animals."

"And what is he looking for?" I asked, when we had parted from him.

"A beast with five fingers," said Saunders. "This afternoon, since he has been in the reptile house, I suppose it will be a reptile with a hand. Next week it will be a monkey with practically no body. The poor old chap is a born materialist.

---

[1] Today we refer to them in the shortened form: zoo.

"It's a queer coincidence, by the way, that you should have known Adrian Borlsover and that you should have received a blessing at his hand. Has it brought you any luck?"

"No," I answered slowly, as I looked back over a life of inconspicuous failure, "I don't think it has. It was his right hand, you know."

HONORARY HEATHEN

**. . . SOMETHING
BLACK AND CHARRED
WAS CREEPING SLOWLY,
VERY SLOWLY, FROM
THE MASS OF FLAMES . . .**